MORE
Night Frights

D1125192

MORE

Night Frights

THIRTEEN SCARY STORIES

J.B. STAMPER

AN
APPLE
PAPERBACK

SCHOLASTIC INC.
New York Toronto London Auckland Sydney

*Some stories are retellings of classic
American folklore legends.*

ISBN 0-590-46045-5

12 11 10 9 8 7 6 ˻   4 5 6 7 8/9

Printed in the U.S.A.   40

First Scholastic printing, September 1993

Contents

MORE
Night Frights

The Vampire's Grave

The four boys met in the town park after dinner to play ball and hang around together. It didn't take long for their conversation to turn to the funeral that had taken place in town that day. Everyone had been talking about it.

The corpse was that of a stranger who had moved into town only a month ago. The man had bought a big Victorian house that had sat empty for years. His name was Mr. Von Dram, and he was different from everyone else in the town. He drove a long black car and wore expensive black suits everywhere he went. Gossips whispered that he had become rich through illegal means. But the kids in town had another theory. They thought he was a vampire.

"It even looked like a vampire funeral," Mike said as the four friends sat down to talk under a big oak tree.

"Did you see that black coffin?" Tim asked. "It

1

must have cost a fortune — and it was as big as a bed."

"I'll bet he's not really dead in there," Kevin added. "I'll bet he's just resting . . . waiting to wake up at midnight and find another victim."

"You guys sound like a bunch of old women," Brian said. "Von Dram is dead as a doornail. He's buried six feet under right now. All that talk about him being a vampire is ridiculous. I don't believe a word of it."

The other three boys stopped talking and just stared at Brian for a few minutes. He was a braggart who was always trying to act braver and better than everybody else.

"I've got an idea, Brian," Kevin finally said. "If you think you're so smart, why don't you just go into the graveyard tonight and visit Von Dram's grave?"

"Yeah, we dare you," Tim added.

"And you can drive a stake right into his grave, just to prove you were there," Mike said. "We'll all go in tomorrow morning to find it."

Brian was silent for awhile. Then, in an arrogant voice, he announced, "Okay, I'll do it. The graveyard doesn't scare me. And Von Dram is just as dead as the rest of the people in it."

Mike jumped up and snapped off a thick dead branch from the oak tree. "I'll make the stake right now," he said. He pulled out his pocketknife

2

and started to whittle the end of the stick into a sharp point. Then he handed the stake to Brian.

"These are the rules," he said. "You go in alone at midnight. You drive this stake into Von Dram's grave — if you're brave enough. And tomorrow morning, we'll all come back to see that you've done it."

Brian grabbed the stake out of his friend's hand and laughed. "Don't worry, you'll find the stake right through that vampire's grave in the morning."

With those words, the boys split up, each going home to his house, since twilight had fallen over the town.

When midnight came, Brian crept out of his bedroom and grabbed one of his father's old jackets from a peg by the back door. Then he ran away from his house toward the graveyard. He wasn't really afraid, but he didn't feel as brave as he had when he had boasted to his friends in the park. The night was cold and he had to zip up his father's big jacket and wrap it around him to keep from shivering.

In the jacket pocket he carried the stake that Mike had sharpened into a point. Brian couldn't help thinking about that sharp point and how it might even go through the coffin lid when he pounded it into the grave. He had also brought along an old wooden mallet that he'd found in the basement of his house. He knew he might need the mallet to pound the stake really deep into the ground.

When he got to the graveyard, Brian easily jumped over the low stone fence that surrounded it. He tried not to think about where he was and just kept on walking through the tombstones to where he knew Mr. Von Dram had been buried that morning. The tombstones shone eerily in the moonlight, looking like ghosts rising up around him.

As he got closer and closer to the freshly dug grave, Brian started to think about Mr. Von Dram. He remembered his pale, sickly complexion and his dark, burning eyes. Maybe he just looked that way because he was sick. Or was it because he was really a vampire? Suddenly, Brian imagined the dead man rising up out of his grave. He might be hiding behind his tombstone right now, his fangs bared, waiting for a victim.

The thought made Brian stop dead in his tracks. But he shook his head to clear his thoughts and forced his legs to walk on. His friends' stories had just gotten to him. He didn't believe in vampires, and he wasn't going to lose this dare.

A few minutes later, he came up to the grave. The moonlight shone down on the name on the huge tombstone: VON DRAM. Brian knelt down on the cool earth that covered the grave. It didn't look as smooth as he thought it would. Had something just disturbed it? Brian felt fear creep through his body. He knelt down and quickly stabbed the sharpened end of the stake into the ground over the grave. Then, he took the mallet and began pounding the stake into the ground. With each swing of the mallet, he thought about the body lying under the ground. What if it was a vampire? What if he woke it up with his pounding? What if it suddenly came out of the grave and tried to grab him and sink its fangs into his neck?

Brian gave the stake one final hit and then tested to see that it was securely in the ground. The stake was pounded in so deep that he knew it must be close to the coffin lid. Then Brian started to jump up to run back home. But he couldn't move! Something was holding onto him! It pulled and tugged at his body, dragging him toward the grave. Fear blotted out all of Brian's thoughts except one: The vampire had risen out of the grave. It wanted to get him!

The next morning, the other three boys woke up early and met at the graveyard. They jumped over the fence and ran as fast as they could to where Mr. Von Dram had been buried. They were taking bets on whether or not they would find the stake driven into the grave. But when they came up to the freshly dug grave, they saw a limp body lying on top of it.

It was Brian, his face twisted in terror. Then they saw the stake that he had pounded through the bottom edge of his father's jacket. He had pinned himself to the grave. And he had died of fright.

The Hook

The four boys huddled around the camp fire, trying to stay warm. It was a late summer night that had turned suddenly cold, much colder than normal for that time of year. The younger boys were shivering because they hadn't thought to bring along jackets. Only Eric, the lead scout, seemed warm enough.

"What's the matter with you guys?" Eric asked. "You act as though you've never camped before. Maybe I shouldn't have brought you up to the mountains. I thought you were tough enough for this trip."

"We're tough enough," Brian said. "It's just freezing, that's all. Why didn't you tell us it would be this cold up here?"

"I didn't know it would be this cold," Eric snapped back. "Anyway, you're supposed to be prepared for anything."

"I'm not prepared to freeze to death," Mark muttered.

"Why can't we go home?" Todd asked, his voice trembling. It was his first camp-out.

"I'm not going home — no matter how much you whine," Eric said. "And remember, I'm the only one who can drive. Besides, I've got the keys to the van." He pulled the keys out of his pocket and dangled them in front of the other boys' eyes.

"Can we tell stories?" Mark asked. "Maybe that would take our minds off freezing to death."

"No stories tonight," Eric said.

"Why not?" Doug asked. "You always tell stories, scary ones."

"This place gives me the creeps bad enough without scary stories," Eric said. "If you want to tell stories yourself, go ahead. I'll turn in."

The four younger boys looked at each other across the leaping flames of the camp fire. For a while, everyone was quiet.

"What gives you the creeps about this place?" Brian finally asked in a low voice.

Eric didn't answer right away. He looked up at the towering fir trees that circled the camp fire. Their ragged limbs were flapping up and down in the cold wind. The other boys watched him. Then they all stared at each other across the fire.

"It's because of a news report I heard on the

8

way up here," Eric said. "You know how they always make things sound like a big deal on the radio."

Todd started to shiver harder. "Why don't we just go home?" he pleaded.

"What was the news report?" Mark asked in a hushed voice. The woods around them had suddenly seemed to grow more quiet and mysterious.

"It was on that prison about twenty miles down the road," Eric said.

The younger boys stared at him. No one had told them about the prison before.

"And the news report said," Eric went on, "that one of the convicts escaped. I remember hearing about him when he was finally caught and put away. They call him the Hook."

"Why do they call him that?" Brian asked right away.

"He lost his left hand in an accident," Eric explained. "And he has a hook there instead of a hand."

"I want to go home," Todd said, louder now.

"Did the radio say which way he was heading?" Mark asked.

"No," Eric answered with a grim look on his face. "They just said that he was dangerous."

No one said anything for a while. They just sat around the fire listening to the wind whip through the trees and moan across the sides of the mountain. Finally, Eric got up and said he was packing it in for the night. He told the younger boys to kill the fire and then get into their tent. Eric had a tent of his own, but the others were sharing a big tent for four.

The boys doused the flames of the fire, threw dirt on it, and then went off to their tent. Each of them had his own private thoughts that he didn't want to admit to the others.

But when they crawled into their sleeping bags, away from Eric, they started to talk about him — the Hook.

"If he's so dangerous, what are we doing out here?" Mark said. "I think Eric is either lying to us, or he's just plain crazy."

"I remember reading about the Hook in the papers, a couple of years ago. He's a murderer," Doug said.

"I want to go home," Todd said with an edge of panic in his voice.

Just then, a strange noise came from out of the woods near their tent. It sounded like the scratching of metal against a tree. The four boys turned their fearful eyes toward the tent opening.

"Eric!" Todd began to scream. The three other boys didn't stop him. They wanted Eric to come, too.

A few minutes later, Eric threw open the tent flap. His eyes looked scared.

"Did you hear it, Eric?" Brian asked. "It sounded like, like . . ."

"Let's get out of here," Eric said. "We can come back for our stuff later."

The boys scrambled out of the tent and ran after Eric to the van. They jumped inside and slammed the doors shut, pushing down the locks as Eric turned the key and the engine roared to life.

Just as the van lurched forward, they heard the sound of something scraping against the side of the van. Then there was a weird-sounding scream as Eric gunned the motor and the van shot off down the forest road.

No one spoke until they were out of the woods and traveling along the main road toward home. No one wanted to talk about the terrible thoughts running through their minds. Finally, Eric broke the silence when he saw a gas station ahead.

"I think we're far enough away," he said. "I've got to fill up the tank."

As the van rolled to a stop in front of the gas pumps, the boys slowly opened the doors to get out. It was Todd who saw it first. He stepped out and looked at the door handle on his side of the van. Then he started to scream. Something was hanging from the handle, swinging back and forth, back and forth.

It was a hook.

Two Dead Eyes

One night, in the middle of a terrible storm, a bolt of lightning struck the big house where a very rich old woman lived. It was the worst streak of lightning that anyone had ever seen, followed by the loudest clap of thunder that anyone had ever heard. And the next morning, the servants found the old woman sitting straight up in bed, her eyes wide open in fright. She was dead.

It frightened the servants to see her two dead eyes, staring at them in terror. They tried to close the lids over the eyes, but each time they tried, the eyes would open back up and stare right through them.

Soon, the old woman's relatives arrived and started to prepare for the funeral. They bought the woman the best coffin made. They had her grave dug on the highest spot in the cemetery. And they chose the most beautiful dress for her to be buried in. The undertaker was given strict instructions to shut her eyes for the funeral, but try as he might, he couldn't get the two dead eyes to stay shut.

Finally, the old woman's cousin had an idea. He found two of the gold coins the woman had been so fond of collecting. Gently, he shut her lids and then laid a coin over each eye. The weight of the heavy gold coins kept the two dead eyes shut.

The family thought the woman looked rather strange with the two gold coins lying on her face, looking like round yellow eyes. But they all agreed that it was better that they didn't have to look at her real eyes, staring at them, as they closed the lid to the coffin. The funeral service was carried out, and the coffin taken to the grave-yard.

After the family left the graveyard, the under-taker turned the coffin over to the gravedigger to do his job. The gravedigger had heard about the two gold coins that were holding the dead woman's eyes shut. As soon as he was left alone in the graveyard, a wave of curiosity swept over him. What did those coins look like? Were they really as thick and heavy as he had heard they were?

The gravedigger crawled down into the grave and then peeked up over the top to make sure that no one was watching him. Then he stooped down, brushed off the small amount of dirt that had been thrown on top of the coffin, pried open the coffin lid, and lifted it off.

As he looked down on the old woman's face, a ray of sunlight flashed off the two gold coins, almost blinding him. The gravedigger staggered back, and then gazed down in amazement at the heavy gold circles shining on the woman's face. He decided they must be worth a fortune, in their weight of gold alone. Quickly, he calculated all the things he could buy with that gold. He could be a rich man! Almost automatically, his hands reached out for the two gold coins. He plucked both of them off the woman's face at the same time, feeling their cool, heavy weight in his hands.

But the moment he lifted up the coins, the woman's eyelids flew open, and her two dead eyes stared up into the gravedigger's face. A stab of fear struck deep in his heart. Those two dead eyes seemed to be accusing him. They stared and stared and stared at him, never flickering, never blinking.

The gravedigger couldn't stand to look at the eyes any longer. He slammed shut the coffin lid and pushed the two gold coins down into his jacket pocket. Then, like a madman, he began to shovel dirt over the coffin until it was buried deep under the ground. Only when he was finished did he stop to take out the gold coins from his pocket and admire them.

As soon as the gravedigger got home, he hid the gold coins in an old metal box that he kept under his bed. All the time he was taking the coins out of his pocket and putting them in the box, he felt as though someone was watching him. But he knew it was just his imagination. No one had been in the cemetery when he took the coins, and he lived all alone in his little house deep in the woods.

That night, another storm came up just like the one that had scared the old woman to death. The wind howled through the trees around the gravedigger's house and shook the wooden walls. The gravedigger huddled under the blankets of his bed, shivering with cold. Then he heard a strange sound that made him shake even harder. It was a rattle, a rattle of metal beneath his bed.

Clink. Clink. Clinkity-clink.

The gravedigger sat straight up in bed, his eyes staring into the darkness in front of him. What was that noise? He strained his ears to hear.

Clink. Clink. Clinkity-clink.

The sound was coming from beneath his bed. There was only one thing that it could be. The two gold coins from the woman's eyes were rattling in the metal box where he had hidden them.

Clink. Clink. Clinkity-clink.

The gravedigger slowly lay back down in his bed and shut his eyes. It must be the wind making the metal box shake, he decided. But then he heard a sound on the wind, a sound like a low, moaning voice.

"Whoooo? Whoooo took my gold coins?"

The gravedigger sat bolt upright in his bed again. The coins were shaking and rattling beneath him. And the spooky voice was coming closer and closer through the night.

"Whoooo? Whooo took my gold coins?"

The gravedigger pulled the blankets around him tighter and started to shake as hard as the coins in the metal box.

Suddenly, the front door blew open and a gust of wind rushed through the house and ripped the blankets right off the gravedigger. He huddled against the head of his bed and stared at the open doorway. Then he saw them. The two dead eyes. They were coming toward him through the dark. They seemed to be burning with anger and evil.

The gravedigger tried to shrink into his bed so the eyes couldn't find him. But then the gold coins started to rattle even louder in the metal box beneath him.

Clink. Clink. Clinkity-clink.

The two dead eyes moved toward him faster now. And the voice echoed through the air around him.

16

"Whoooo? Whoooo took my gold coins?"

The gravedigger sat bolt upright in his bed and screamed, "I did!"

And the next morning, people found him just like that — with his two dead eyes staring straight ahead in fright.

The Bloodsucker

No one who saw the bloodsucker ever lived to tell about it. So no one knew exactly what he looked like. People said the bloodsucker was an evil ghost that lurked in the dark shadows of the woods waiting for a person to stay in the forest too long, too late. As the light faded from the sky, the bloodsucker would get more and more thirsty. He could smell human blood from miles away. And when he found a victim, he would swoop out from the dark shadows — and suck every drop of blood out of the person's body.

One day, a boy who lived in the woods — his name was Adam — had to deliver a horse to a man who lived miles away. Adam had set off early in the day, but the journey took much longer than he had expected. By the time he had delivered the horse and begun his walk back home, the shadows of the woods had grown darker and longer.

The birds had stopped chirping and folded their wings for the night.

Adam started walking faster down the forest path, nervously looking up at the twilight sky. He knew he still had an hour's journey to go, and he knew that twilight would never last that long. As Adam hurried along, the thought of the bloodsucker crept into his mind. Just before he'd left home that morning, his older brother, Thomas, had warned him not to travel too slowly. Thomas hadn't mentioned the bloodsucker, but both of them knew what he meant.

Adam started to run down the path, suddenly seeing strange shapes and faces in the forest shadows. The harder he ran, the more his blood began to pound in his veins. Adam reached his hand up to his face and felt the warm blood that had rushed to the surface. He wondered if his blood smelled more strongly now that it was warm. Maybe the smell of it was floating through the woods right now, tempting the bloodsucker.

Adam felt tears spring to his eyes, and he tried to run faster. But his breath was coming in short, painful gasps and, finally, his legs grew so weak that he stumbled over a thick root that snaked across the forest floor. He sprawled out, face down, on the path strewn with sharp pine needles. For a moment he lay there exhausted, too tired to move.

Finally, he turned over and looked up at the shadowy trees looming above him. Then he heard a strange noise, a noise like he'd never heard before. It was coming toward him, closer and closer and louder and louder. It was the sound of something huge, sucking in the air. Adam raised himself up on his elbow, terrified by the sound, but too weak to escape. Then, just as he saw the bloodsucker swoop down on him, he began to scream.

A minute later, the forest was quiet.

Thomas, his older brother, found Adam's body the next day. It was limp and pale, drained of every drop of blood. There was a trail of blood left by the bloodsucker, leading away into the forest. As Thomas carried his brother's body home, he vowed to get revenge on the bloodsucker.

He took Adam's body home and buried it. Then he began to make his plans. All day, he sharpened the hunting knives that he kept in the barn. That night, just before the light was beginning to fade from the sky, he returned to the forest carrying a heavy load on his back. He found the trail of blood that led away from the spot where the bloodsucker had sucked the life out of Adam's body. He followed it through the darkening forest to the mouth of a cave.

Thomas knew he had to work fast. Twilight was creeping over the sky, and he knew the smell of his own blood would soon be stirring the appetite of the bloodsucker.

He threw the heavy pack onto the ground and pulled the sharpened knives out one by one. Their points glistened in the fading light. He dug the handles of the knives into the ground in front of the cave and pointed the long, sharp blades toward its opening. Then, trembling, he stood still behind the knives while the light grew dimmer and dimmer in the sky.

Just when the outlines of the trees had faded from green to black, Thomas heard a terrifying sound from inside the cave. The blood in his veins began to pound with fear, but he stood his ground behind the knives. Then, suddenly, the bloodsucker swooped out of the cave, its huge mouth gaping open, thirsty for blood.

The bloodsucker came right for Thomas, not seeing the rows of blades in front of him. It screamed out and twisted and turned in agony as the sharp knives cut it into hundreds and thousands of pieces.

Then all those pieces of the bloodsucker flew up into the night sky. And they turned into mosquitoes, still thirsty for blood.

And, so, if you're ever out in the woods at night, watch out for mosquitoes. They'll suck the blood right out of you!

Time Was Running Out

The human mind starts acting strangely after a person has been alone for a long time. That's what I tried to tell myself as I lay in my bed, tossing and turning. It had to be my imagination, I said over and over. That sound I heard . . . that tapping, tocking sound.

I was all alone in the North Woods. For ten days I had been ice fishing during the day and then writing in my journal at night. The cold weather and bleak landscape around me was the sort of break I needed from my high-pressure job in the city. Everything had been peaceful and quiet — until now. Now my mind was obsessed by the sound that I had been hearing for what seemed like hours — the sound of something tapping on the lake ice that surrounded my cabin on nearly all sides.

I got out of bed and peered out the window of my cabin. It was dawn and the sun was just coloring the sky with pale blues and pinks. I thought I saw a dark figure moving across the ice toward my cabin, but then it seemed to disappear. I wasn't sure if I had imagined seeing it or not.

I pulled on my long underwear and hunting clothes — parka, insulated pants, boots, fur cap, and gloves. I wasn't sure what I was going to do, but I knew I couldn't just sit in my cabin any longer, waiting for the tapping noise to come to me. If I did, I'd go crazy.

I slipped outside and gulped in breaths of the icy cold air. Outside, the sound was even louder. As I listened to it echoing across the frozen lake, I suddenly realized what must be causing it. A person was coming toward me, testing the ice with a pole. Each time the pole was set down against the hard surface of the ice, it made a tapping sound.

A wave of relief washed over me, but it was soon replaced by an uneasy curiosity about who might be coming toward me in this isolated wilderness. Who was it? And why did he want to find me?

Instinctively, I sought cover in a stand of huge fir trees. I wanted to see who was making the noise before being seen myself. I waited there, for what seemed like an hour, listening as the tapping, tocking sound grew closer and closer. Finally, I realized that my fingers and toes had grown numb and stiff. I was risking frostbite if I remained still any longer. I stepped out from the cover of the trees. Gazing across the frozen lake around me, I couldn't see anyone. But now I heard the sound moving in a different direction — away from me. Somehow, the person tapping his pole on the ice had circled around me and was now moving away.

Forgetting that I hadn't eaten breakfast or supplied myself with food, I began to trail the mysterious sound. Even though it was moving away from me now, I feared it even more. It had an evil persistence that drilled into my brain. I had to know what person was prowling on these lakes — I didn't want to be surprised by a sudden intruder in my cabin.

For hours, I followed the tapping and tocking across the ice. It led me in a half circle around the lake. I was beginning to feel hungry and cold, and suddenly, I knew I had to head back to my cabin. If I didn't get there by nightfall, I would freeze to death on the lake.

I came to a halt on the ice, my legs trembling with fatigue. And as I turned my back to begin my walk home, my blood turned even colder than before. I realized that, now, the tapping sound was following me. It was tracking me down across the ice.

Panic began to seep through my body. It made

me feel weaker than before, but I started to run anyway. Before, I had been curious, and then fearful, of the sound; now I was terrified.

Tock. Tock. Tock.

The sound seemed to grow louder and louder in my ears. I staggered across the icy lake, no longer checking for the thin places in the ice where warmer currents ran. I knew only one thing. I had to escape that sound before it caught up with me.

Tock. Tock. Tock.

Suddenly, I sprawled forward onto the ice. My legs had given out. I was starving and could feel the frostbite creeping into my fingers and toes. But the sound of the tapping, tocking pole didn't stop. It came closer and closer, hunting me down like a predator's victim.

Tock. Tock. Tock.

In my mind, I could see who must be carrying that pole. His face was covered by a bushy black beard. His eyes were evil and hungry. His ragged teeth worked hungrily under red lips. I lay on the ice, unable to move. I knew it was only a matter of time until the tocking sound reached my face, frozen against the ice. And time was running out.

"No!" I screamed. And I sat bolt upright. Looking around me, I saw the warm, wooden walls of the cabin where I was staying in the North Woods.

But the sound, that dreadful sound, was still there.

I turned around and saw the old-fashioned clock hanging on the wall over my bed. It was ticking and tocking, ticking and tocking — its sound still tapping at my feverish brain.

Over the Hill

The scout troop had settled for the night in a valley between two large hills. A small creek ran through the valley near where they had set up camp. And the hills that crept up to the sky on both sides of it were covered with thick, dark trees. The two scout leaders, who were still teenagers, had never camped in this place before. But the trail leading into the valley had been easy to follow, and so they had led their group of ten younger scouts down to this spot.

The two leaders, Matt and John, were good scouts, but they weren't too concerned about the younger boys they had brought along on this camping trip. They had been stuck with the job after the senior scout leader had suddenly fallen ill. And so they let the younger boys take care of themselves while they sat around the fire and talked over their plans for what they would do after high school graduation.

One of the younger scouts, named Ben, came up and interrupted them. "Matt, what's on the other side of that hill?" he asked, pointing to the hill that lay on the other side of the valley from where they had come.

"No idea," Matt answered. "I've never been here before."

"Will we go there tomorrow?" Ben asked.

"No, we're turning right back around and going home," Matt said, "soon as you guys wake up."

"But what are we going to do tonight?" Ben asked, persistently. "This is boring, just sitting around."

Several of the other younger scouts had gathered behind Ben. They wanted to tell stories, or sing songs, or do anything but sit in their tents.

"Listen, Ben, if you're so bored, why don't you go over the hill?" John said, half as a joke. "You can take your flashlight and explore. How about it?"

"Okay, I'll do it," Ben answered. He looked a little scared, but he wasn't going to admit it to his friends.

Matt and John settled back to their conversation, not really paying any attention to what Ben was doing. The other boys watched from the campsite as Ben walked along the trail that led up the hill. They could see his flashlight beam climbing higher and higher up. It quavered a bit at the very top of the hill, and then disappeared as he went over the hill and down the other side.

The younger scouts sat and watched the spot on the top of the hill where Ben's light had disappeared. But it never came back. They sat and watched for twenty minutes. Then Leroy went to the camp fire to talk to the two leaders.

"Ben didn't come back," he said. "Somebody had better check on him."

Matt and John thought he was kidding. They didn't really want to be bothered, anyway.

"So, go find him," Matt said.

Leroy got his flashlight and set off on the trail up from the valley. The other scouts watched as the beam of his flashlight moved slowly up the hill. Leroy stopped several times and seemed to think about turning back. But then his flashlight beam traveled back upwards until, finally, it reached the top of the hill. It shone there for a few seconds, and then disappeared.

The boys waited for fifteen minutes. But Leroy's light never appeared again. This time, the rest of the eight boys went to the camp fire. They told Matt and John what had happened.

"Come on, they're just playing a game with you," John said. "Somebody always tries to pull something like this on a camping trip. You wait long enough, and they'll be sneaking back into camp to scare you."

29

The eight scouts went back to the place near their tents where they could stare up at the spot on the hill where they had last seen Ben's and Leroy's lights. They waited and waited, but the hill remained as dark as ever, a hulking shadow against the night sky.

Finally, the boys walked up to Matt and John again.

"We're going over the hill," one of them said, "to find Ben and Leroy."

"We'll watch you," Matt said, laughing. "And don't stay out too late."

The eight boys lined up with their flashlights and then began walking up the hill. From the camp fire in the valley, Matt and John could see the eight beams of their flashlights flickering and moving slowly up the trail. Every so often, the lights would stop, and then move on again. When the line of eight lights had almost reached the top of the hill, they suddenly began to come back down again, fast — as though the boys were running. But then they stopped, and slowly, like a funeral procession, began to move back upwards again. The lights reached the top and then went over the hill. And disappeared from sight.

Matt and John sat around the camp fire for another hour, talking and laughing. Then they began to get worried. Maybe this wasn't a prank after all. Maybe, they began to think, they should have taken better care of the younger scouts.

They got out their big lanterns, lit them, and then walked up the hill. On the way up, they searched every inch of the trail. When they reached the top, they looked over the other side of the hill.

Even in the moonlight, all they could see was blackness — nothing but blackness. They seemed to be looking into a big, dark hole that would swallow up anything that went into it. Matt and John called and called the younger boys' names. But no one answered. There wasn't any sound at all. In the morning, they sent out a search party. But no one ever found the ten scouts.

They had gone over the hill.

The Hitchhiker

One evening, at twilight, a man was driving along a lonely country road toward a town he'd never visited before. He was on a business trip, and he was watching the road signs carefully to see where he was going. The countryside around him was hilly and covered with pine trees. It was the kind of country that made him feel uneasy, because he'd grown up in the city. Like many city people, he found more to be afraid of in wide-open spaces that he did on crowded streets.

The shadows of the tall trees were growing longer and darker when he came to a fork where the road split in two different directions. The man peered at his map, but couldn't find this place anywhere on it. A feeling of panic began to grow in his mind as he looked down one of the desolate roads and then the other. It seemed that neither one led anywhere, and now the sky was turning a dark, inky blue.

Just then, a figure appeared only a few feet from his car door. It appeared so quickly that it seemed to come out of nowhere. The man quickly locked his car doors, and then watched nervously as the figure came closer. He saw that it was a woman, a young woman, and she seemed to be frightened, too. As she came closer to the car, he rolled down the window.

"Please, sir," she pleaded in a breathless voice. "Could you give me a ride?"

The man looked at her with sympathy. She was obviously harmless, he thought, and she needed help. Besides, he told himself, she would be able to direct him to the town he was looking for.

"Where can I take you?" he asked the young woman. "You look lost, too."

"Oh, no, I'm not lost," she said. "I live quite nearby. It's just that I need to be someplace soon, and I am too tired to walk."

The man told the young woman to get into the car, and that he would take her where she needed to go. After sitting down in the front seat, she directed him to take the left fork of the road and to drive on for about four miles.

Before starting off down the road, the man looked over at his passenger and noticed the paleness of her skin and the trembling of her hands. He wondered if she had just had a shock. But she didn't answer his questions about how she felt. She just asked him to please hurry. She had to be somewhere and had no time to waste.

The man began driving down the road to the left, glancing over at the young woman from time to time. The light was fading rapidly from the sky, but he could still see her clearly. As they drove on and it became darker, it seemed to him that her face was becoming thinner and thinner. Her eyes, when they met his, seemed to become darker and stared out from deep bony sockets in her face.

Suddenly, the man felt a tremor of fear pass through his body. He still had no idea where he was going. And this young woman was very strange.

"Will this road take me on to Wilsonville?" he asked, hoping that her answer would be yes.

"Oh, no," the young woman answered in a voice that suddenly sounded as thin and dry as old paper. "You'll have to turn around after you drop me off. Wilsonville is on the road that forks to the right."

Looking over at her in irritation, the man was shocked to see that her face looked almost like a skull, with bare teeth grinning at him. He quickly stared back at the road, telling himself that the light was bad and his imagination was getting the better of him.

A few minutes later, the young woman called out for him to stop. He braked on top of a hill and saw the white tombstones of a cemetery glowing in the moonlight on both sides of the road. Then he heard the car door open. And as he looked over to where his passenger had been, he saw a skeleton stepping away from the car into the cemetery.

The man didn't waste any time turning the car around and racing back down the road to the fork. No sooner had he pulled onto the road that went to the right than he saw the wreck of an automobile. It had exploded into flames and was burnt almost beyond recognition. A policeman was standing beside it, shaking his head as the man pulled up.

"Nothing could be done to save her," the policeman said. "She's among the dead now."

"I know," the man answered. "I just took her ghost to the graveyard."

The Blue Coffin

They say twins have a special way of communicating with each other — almost as if their two minds are one. This was true of the Jones twins from the minute they were born. If one started to cry as a baby, the other seemed to sense its pain and cry, too. As children, Mary and Maggie Jones learned to speak and read and add at the same time. Their two minds were like copies of each other and, often, they didn't need to speak in order to know what the other was thinking.

The two girls grew up to be identical in all ways — until they turned sixteen, that is. A month after their sixteenth birthday, Maggie suddenly became ill. It was a slow, creeping illness, the kind that no one even noticed at first. But the young girl lost weight, week after week, and soon her arms and legs were thin and spindly. Her face lost its rosy blush and took on a pale, grayish cast. Mary, meanwhile, stayed strong and healthy.

The parents took Maggie to doctor after doctor, but none of them could determine what illness she had. And none of them found a medicine or cure that could stop it. Sometimes, when she looked at her sick sister, Mary would suddenly be overcome by the same feeling of weakness that Maggie felt. She wanted to be able to give her own strength to Maggie, but not even she could help her sister.

After six months of getting weaker and weaker, Maggie stopped breathing one morning. Mary found her, lying quiet and still in her bed. To Mary, she didn't seem dead, just trapped in a very deep sleep. In fact, she seemed to still sense Maggie's feelings inside her own mind.

When their parents looked at Maggie, they began to cry and called the doctor. They knew she had to be dead, because she was not breathing and her pulse showed no sign of life. When the doctor came and examined the girl's limp, lifeless body, he confirmed their fears. Maggie had finally died of her mysterious illness.

Mary took the death worse than anyone. She sat by Maggie's bedside hour after hour, holding her hand. In fact, she refused to believe that her twin had died. Her parents had to lock her in her room when Maggie's body was taken away.

At the funeral, Mary looked down at Maggie in her favorite blue dress, lying on the blue satin of the coffin. Blue had been her favorite color and now she would be surrounded by it forever. The strange feeling that Maggie was still alive kept haunting Mary. But looking at the pale face with its grayish cast, she could see that was impossible. She felt as though part of herself had died, and she almost wished that she were lying beside Maggie in the coffin. Maggie looked at peace — while Mary felt tormented by her death.

They buried Maggie in the town graveyard that was only a block from the Joneses' house. That night, Mary fell asleep haunted by nightmares of being buried in that blue coffin under six feet of cold hard ground. Her parents sat beside Mary's bed until they knew that she was finally asleep. Then they went to their own bed to let sleep ease their grief.

Much later, in the middle of the night, they heard a terrible cry come from Mary's room. *Aaaaaaaaagggghhh!* She was screaming and screaming with terror. They rushed to her bedside, and saw her twisting and turning in her bed and clawing at the air above her.

"Let me out," she screamed. "Let me out!"

Her father shook Mary to wake her up. But then he realized that she was awake already, and she was still screaming and begging to be let out.

"Mary, Mary, what's the matter?" her mother asked.

"It's Maggie, she's alive," Mary sobbed. "She's alive in that blue coffin."

Her parents tried to comfort and calm Mary, but she would not be silenced.

"I can feel it," Mary said. "She wants out of that coffin. She can't breathe."

The parents didn't know what to do. They understood how close the twins had been. And the doctor had warned them that Mary might have a serious emotional reaction to Maggie's death.

"Mary, you must get those thoughts out of your mind," her father said. "Maggie is dead."

"No, she's not," Mary said. "She's trying to stay alive, but she can't breathe in that coffin."

Then Mary started to claw wildly at the air in front of her again.

Her mother began to sob, now half believing what Mary was saying. She began to beg her husband to go to the graveyard. Mary jumped up from her bed and got dressed.

"We have to save her, before it's too late," she cried.

The family rushed to the garage to get shovels and then drove through the night to the graveyard. With Mary in the lead, they ran to Maggie's grave and began to dig and shovel and dig and shovel the dirt that lay cold and heavy over Maggie's coffin. When they finally uncovered it, Mr.

Jones, with trembling hands, unlocked the coffin lid and lifted it up. By the light of the moon, they looked down into the blue coffin.

Maggie lay still in her coffin bed. She was finally dead. Her face was twisted in agony, as though she had fought and fought for breath and lost the battle. Her long, thin fingers were ragged and bloody from having scratched at the top of the coffin.

And the lid of the blue coffin, where she had been buried alive, was carved with deep marks from her frantic fingers.

The Bogey

"**H**ave they told you about the Bogey yet?" Jeffrey felt his body tense. Kenny's whispering voice was so close to his ear that it sounded like a snake hissing. Kenny slept in the bunk next to his, and their heads were only inches apart.

"Be quiet," Jeffrey whispered back. "I'm trying to sleep."

"You don't know about him, do you?" Kenny sounded determined to talk, even though it was against the rules after lights out.

"So what if I don't?" Jeffrey said. "It sounds like a scary story."

"Listen, this is your first year at Camp Cypress," Kenny said. "You don't know half the stuff that goes on around here."

Jeffrey felt the hair stand up on the back of his neck. Kenny had just made him remember the creepy feeling he'd had when he first came to Camp Cypress, four days ago. It wasn't like the

41

other camps he'd gone to. It was on the edge of a swamp. And it was more isolated and run down. Even his parents had looked a little nervous about leaving him.

"This place used to be an old private hideout," Kenny said in a low voice. "If you look around, you can find old coins and things."

Jeffrey lay in the darkness, breathing in and out nervously. He knew Kenny was going to tell him about the Bogey, even if he didn't want to hear it.

"About two hundred years ago," Kenny went on, "a pirate named Captain Bogey made his hideout here. He buried the treasure he'd stolen from hundreds of ships. But his first mate double crossed him. He shot Captain Bogey and stole the treasure. The captain slowly bled to death. But before he died, he vowed that his ghost would come back for revenge. And that's the Bogey. He still wanders through the swamp at night, carrying his knife. And he's still looking for revenge."

Jeffrey lay in the darkness, listening to his heart pound. He knew the story about the Bogey couldn't be true. But, still, he didn't like to think about it. The trees around Camp Cypress were so dark and thick. And, every night, the counselor of their cabin, Peter, made one of the campers go out in the middle of the night and get one of the charred logs from the camp bonfire — just to prove he wasn't afraid to do it. Of the boys in the cabin, four had already gone. That left only Kenny and himself for tonight.

As Jeffrey lay there in the dark, he heard Peter clear his throat from across the cabin. A nervous chill ran down his spine. That's what Peter always did just before he woke everybody up for the nightly test — the coward test, he called it.

"Ready to go tonight?" Kenny whispered in Jeffrey's ear with a snicker. "It's either you or me, and I already did it last year."

Jeffrey felt the nervous twinge in the pit of his stomach begin to spread throughout his body. He told himself that Kenny's story was just a joke. But the idea of the Bogey had begun to grow real in his mind.

"It's time for the test," Peter suddenly called out in his low voice that had an edge of meanness to it. Jeffrey heard the rest of the boys in the cabin groan and yawn. Everyone was getting used to Peter's trick of waking them up, but they still didn't like it. "Jeffrey, get up!" Peter's voice ordered. "You're taking a little walk tonight."

A rush of fear shot through Jeffrey's body, leaving his arms and legs feeling weak and heavy as stone. He struggled out of his bunk and pulled on a sweatshirt and his jeans.

"You know what you have to do, Jeffrey. You go through the swamp to where the big bonfire was tonight. The trail is pretty dark this time of night, isn't it, guys?"

The voices of the four boys who had already done the test answered back with scary sounds.

"You pick up one of the charred logs from the bonfire, and then you come back here with it to prove you're not a coward."

Jeffrey swallowed hard and slipped his feet into his sneakers. He knew he couldn't refuse to go. That would brand him as a coward for the rest of the time he was at camp. As he headed for the door, Peter hissed in a low voice, "Don't let the Bogey get you."

Jeffrey stepped out onto the dark path that led away from the cabin to the bonfire site. He could hear the croaking of the frogs from the swamp. In the distance, he could see the other cabins of the camp. He wondered if any of the campers in the other cabins had to do the test. Or was it just Peter's sick idea?

Jeffrey squinted into the darkness ahead of him, trying to make out the trail through the dark trees. There was only a thin sliver of a moon to guide him, and he began to grope his way in the dark, feeling the trees along the sides of the narrow path.

A sudden sound made Jeffrey freeze in his tracks. It came again, a soft, scuffling noise from behind him. An animal, he told himself. He started

44

down the path again, moving more quickly, trying to escape the sound that padded along behind him. But it kept following him, not sounding like an animal anymore. It sounded like . . . the Bogey.

The soggy earth of the trail suddenly came to an end at the bonfire, and Jeffrey rushed over to the cold embers. He felt around until he found one of the charred logs. And, then, he heard the soft thud of footsteps behind him. He clutched the log in his hands and jumped up, sensing the presence of something only inches away.

He whirled around and began to run back down the trail to the cabin. But the footsteps found him in the dark and followed closely behind, like evil shadows. Through the panic in his mind, Jeffrey thought about the sound of the footsteps. Their sound was muffled and soft. They came after him, slowly closing the distance between them, no matter how fast he ran.

"Don't let the Bogey get you." Peter's words raced through Jeffrey's mind with every breath he took. Jeffrey knew he was close to the cabin now, but the footsteps were close to him, too.

Then, with a sickening feeling, Jeffrey heard something slice through the air behind him. An intense pain cut through his back — once, twice — and he almost crumpled to the ground. But fear made him stagger on until, finally, he reached the cabin door. He stumbled into the cabin and dropped the log on the floor, panting like a wild animal that had escaped its predator.

Flashlights flicked on, piercing the darkness with beams of light. Jeffrey stood still, in shock, as the boys came out of their bunks.

"The Bogey," he whispered. "It chased me."

Peter laughed, and then Kenny. "There's no such thing as the Bogey, you fool," Peter said. "That was just a story — to scare you."

"The Bogey got me," Jeffrey gasped. Then his knees buckled and he dropped forward onto the floor in a faint. The other boys gathered around and shone their flashlights down onto his fallen body.

And then they saw it. On his back were two slashes in the form of an X — marked by Captain Bogey.

Night Creature

The family started off down the trail that led to the cabin they had rented deep in the woods. The cabin was deeper into the wilderness than they had ever been before. Not even the father was sure how far they had to walk from where they parked the car to the cabin. He had rented the cabin through the mail after answering an ad in a wilderness magazine.

"The woods are different around here," Meg said. "The trees are taller and thicker."

"And it's darker," David added. "Sort of creepy."

"Don't start scaring yourselves already," Mr. Jackson said. "We have a long way to walk yet. You'll feel more at ease once we find the cabin and get settled in."

"Remember, Rex is here to take care of us," Mrs. Jackson said. Rex wagged his tail at the mention of his name and bounded off ahead of

47

them on the trail. He was a hunting dog and loved being in the woods.

The trail wound through the dense woods, farther and farther away from civilization. Mr. Jackson stopped several times to consult the map he had been sent through the mail. It was just a hand-drawn map, and he was beginning to worry about how accurate it was. They had already gone three times as far as he thought they would have to.

A loud howl echoed through the woods ahead of them. They all stopped, recognizing that it was Rex.

"He sounds upset," Meg said. "Maybe he doesn't like it here."

"He's probably smelled a fox or something," Mr. Jackson said, "and wishes he could catch it."

They all hurried on down the trail, feeling uneasy. Within a few minutes, they found Rex. He was standing in front of an old log cabin. The hair on his back was bristling as he prowled back and forth in front of the cabin, sniffing and whimpering.

"I guess this is it," David said, staring at the cabin.

"I don't like it any more than Rex does," Meg said. "It's not what I thought . . . it's scary."

The four of them stared in silence. Some of the logs had decayed over the years and, in places, a green fungus was growing over the wood. There were four small windows with glass panes, but they were scratched and blurred with age. The worst thing was the door. It was hanging loose from its hinges and standing wide open.

"Well, I guess I won't need the key they sent me in the mail," Mr. Jackson said, trying to sound lighthearted. "Let's go in."

But as the four moved toward the cabin, Rex loped over in front of the doorway and growled.

"He doesn't want us to go in," Meg said. "I think we should get out of here."

Mr. and Mrs. Jackson looked at each other with worried expressions. "It's too late to leave, kids," Mrs. Jackson said. "It'll be dark in an hour. We couldn't possibly make it back to the car on that trail."

Mr. Jackson stepped around Rex and went into the cabin, trying to ignore the dog's growling and whimpering. A few minutes later, he motioned for the rest of the family to come inside.

"It's not so bad," David said as he walked inside and looked around at the one-room cabin. "Except for the smell."

The smell was strange — a mixture of mold and animal scent. Mrs. Jackson went to the windows right away and pulled them open. "Well, at least there are cots for us to sleep on," she said. "After all, we just have to make it through the night. We can leave in the morning if we want to, can't we?" She gave her husband a pleading look.

"We'll see how it goes tonight," he said.

Everyone got busy unpacking their backpacks. The horrible smell seemed to lessen as the wind from the woods blew through the cabin. By the time they all had eaten a meal cooked on their camp stove outside, everyone was in better spirits.

"I wish Rex would stop prowling around and whimpering," Meg said. "He makes me nervous. Every time I start to feel relaxed here, I see him sniffing around like something is wrong."

"Don't worry," her father said, "that's just the hunting dog in him. He'll settle down."

But Mr. Jackson was wrong. Even after they had all gotten into their sleeping bags for the night and closed and locked the cabin door, Rex didn't settle down. He kept prowling around the cabin, whimpering and letting out low growls.

Finally, the family fell asleep from exhaustion. But deep in the night, they woke up.

"What was that?" David whispered. They all sat up in the darkness and waited.

A weird cry came through the woods. It didn't sound like any animal they'd ever heard before. The cry was part whine, part moan, and part blood-curdling howl.

"Hurry, shut the windows," Mrs. Jackson said frantically. Everyone sensed the same fear. They didn't know what the sound was coming from. But they didn't want the creature that was making it inside the cabin.

The cry shrieked through the dark woods again as they scrambled out of their sleeping bags and rushed toward the windows. Rex let out a loud bark and then continued to growl, pacing closer and closer to one of the windows.

"Hurry, shut that window!" Mrs. Jackson called to David. But he was too late. Rex took a running leap and jumped through the last open window into the night, barking and growling.

The four of them stood in the dark, trembling. No one made a move to shut the window again. They all wondered what would happen to Rex if he found that creature in the woods.

They waited and worried in the dark. The woods echoed with the creature's weird cry and Rex's snarls and barks. When the dog hadn't come back after two hours, Mr. Jackson finally shut the window. Then they all fell into an exhausted sleep.

The next morning, everyone was awakened by the sound of scratching and whimpering at the door. The sunlight was pouring into the cabin, and the horror of the night before seemed to have all been a nightmare.

But when they opened the door, they saw that Rex had changed. His eyes were glazed over with fear. He walked hunched down with his head hanging. And his coat was white . . . pure white.

It had been black — until he met the creature of the night.

The Thing in
the Back Seat

It was the night after Karen turned sixteen. She had begged her father to let her get a car for her birthday. After hearing her ask again and again, he finally gave in and said yes. They drove to the used car lot right after dinner. Karen had gotten her driver's license just that afternoon, and she drove her father's large sedan cautiously down the road.

They had agreed that the car should not cost much, and that it would not be too sporty or fast. Secretly, Karen hoped that she might find a bright red car, maybe even a convertible, and convince her father to buy it. But she was willing to settle on anything he agreed to buy. After all, what she really wanted was a set of wheels to give her freedom. Freedom to drive away from home and speed down the road with the wind blowing through her hair.

As soon as they drove up to the lot and parked, Karen jumped out of the car and started to walk up and down the rows of used cars. She couldn't help but feel disappointed. Most of them were family cars with four doors, dull colors, and no personality. She couldn't imagine herself behind the wheel of one of these cars, but she kept trying to tell herself that any car was better than no car.

The salesman came up to her father and started to ask questions. A crooked smile came over his face as he listened to what they were looking for. Then, with a flourish of his arm, he waved them toward a brown sedan that had orange upholstery with plastic seat covers. Karen cringed and tried to pull her father away from the car, but he seemed intent on listening to the salesman's pitch. She crept away from the car, deciding that she wouldn't be caught dead in it.

She backed into a red convertible that had a price tag that was ten times what her father had promised to pay. Still, she couldn't resist slipping into the driver's seat. The minute she gripped the wheel in her hands, she knew it was the car she wanted. Then she looked through the windshield and saw her father's frowning face coming toward her. Quickly, she jumped out of the car and walked toward him, not whispering a word about the convertible.

For another hour, they followed the salesman around the lot as he showed them one car after another. One was too expensive, another too ugly, the next too run-down. Karen began to despair of ever getting a car. She walked away from her father and the salesman and started to wander toward the back of the lot. It was the only place she hadn't looked yet, and she was feeling desperate.

Then, like a miracle, she saw the car. It was dark red — something like the color of dried blood — but just bright enough to look sporty. It wasn't a convertible, but it was sleek and low and had the kind of style she liked. And, best of all, the price was just below what she and her father had agreed on. Karen slipped behind the wheel and settled into the leather bucket seat. The minute she put her hands on the steering wheel, she knew it was the car she had to have.

Suddenly, she saw the salesman walking briskly across the lot toward her, shaking his head.

"No, no, no," he said emphatically. "You do not want that car, young lady."

"I'm afraid you're wrong," she answered just as firmly. "It's exactly the car I want."

Her father came up then and saw her sitting behind the wheel. She noticed the smile that spread across his face when he saw the price tag on the car.

"Well, well, why haven't you shown us this beauty before?" he asked the salesman.

"Listen, everyone who buys this car brings it back," the salesman said. "Trust me."

Karen met her father's eyes. She knew that something about the car had caught his fancy as well. Right away, she went to work convincing him that she should have it. Her father opened up the hood and looked at the engine. As far as he could tell, the car was in perfect shape.

"I think we'll buy it," he told the salesman. "I can write out a check tonight."

"You're just wasting your time," the salesman said. "Everybody who buys this car brings it back."

Karen and her father didn't pay any attention to what he said. They paid for the car and Karen drove it off the lot. All the way home, she kept the windows down so the wind could blow through her hair. She felt free, even though the wind was cold and stung her cheeks.

The next day after school, Karen grabbed her set of car keys and ran out to the car. She jumped inside and took off on a road that led out of town. It was a brisk autumn day and when she rolled down the windows, she became chilled by the cool breeze. Reluctantly, she rolled the windows up again and drove on.

Before long, she began to notice a strange smell. It seemed to be coming from the back seat. The longer she drove on smelling that smell, the sicker she felt. It was a sweet rotting smell, a disgusting aroma that reminded her of graveyards. Karen suddenly didn't feel free anymore and quickly turned the car around to go home.

The next day, the same thing happened. She had to roll the windows up because the weather was so cool. When she did, the whole car began to reek with the rotting smell from the back seat. This time, Karen decided to keep driving, even though the smell bothered her. As she went on, the smell got worse and worse and almost seemed to be alive in the back seat. She glanced up at the rearview mirror, and there, staring back at her, were two evil eyes. Karen screamed and whirled around to look in the back seat. But nothing was there — just the horrible smell.

The next day, Karen decided she wouldn't take a drive in her new car. Then her mother asked her to go on an errand to the next town, and Karen was too embarrassed to admit that she was afraid of the car. So she climbed behind the wheel, rolled down the windows even though it was freezing cold out, and started to drive.

For several miles, it seemed that nothing was wrong with the car at all. Karen almost started to feel the sense of freedom again that she'd first experienced when she sat behind the wheel. Then, when she was all alone on the country road, the smell began. It grew and grew until it filled up the back seat. Then Karen took courage and looked into her rearview mirror. The evil eyes were there again, staring at her. They narrowed as she met their gaze. Karen started to scream. Just as she did, a hand reached from the back seat and grabbed her shoulder. She whirled around. But there was nothing there!

Karen slammed down on the brake, and the car screeched to a stop. As she threw open the door, she felt the hand from the back seat grab at her neck. She looked up into the rearview mirror, and the eyes were there, leering at her. With all her strength, she pulled loose and jumped from the car. She ran all the way home, trying to escape the thing in the back seat.

The next day, Karen and her father took the car back to the lot. The salesman shook his head when he saw them. By evening, the car was back in its place at the rear of the lot.

The thing in the back seat was there, too . . . waiting.

Night Bite

Nancy dreaded the overnight camp-out more than anything else. The idea of spending the night in a sleeping bag in the middle of the woods made her sick with fear. She wanted to run away from camp and go home. But she couldn't do that, of course. Her parents expected her to love camp and the great outdoors. If they only knew.

Now here she was, on the camp-out, sitting around the fire listening to the scary stories everyone liked to tell. Stories about ghosts, vampires, and weird creatures that lived in the woods. She hated the stories. But at least they kept her from having to crawl into her damp sleeping bag on the hard ground. Nancy hadn't told anyone why she hated these overnights in the woods so much. It was her secret, and she was afraid to let the other campers know. They were sure to use it against her. You see, she had a terrible fear of insects.

Once, in the cabin, a daddy longlegs spider had

crawled across her bunk. She had watched its long, thin legs pick their way across her sheet, right over her stomach. She had been too terrified to touch it, or brush it away. And she was afraid to scream because the other girls would find out she was scared. She had just lain there, stiff with fright, while the spider pranced across her body. Now, she was in the middle of the woods with no roof, walls, or floor to protect her.

The flames of the camp fire were burning low, and the head counselor finally told everyone it was time to go to sleep. Nancy wished she felt more tired, but her mind was racing . . . imagining the insects that must be creeping around in the woods: spiders, beetles, ticks, every kind of horrible six-legged jumping or squirming creature.

All the other girls had arranged their sleeping bags together so they could talk and tell stories. As usual, Nancy hadn't been included. She had dragged her sleeping bag near everyone else's. But she was still closer to the trees that surrounded the campsite than anyone else. She wanted to complain and ask to be closer to the fire, which would surely keep away any insects coming near it. But she knew it was no use. The counselor didn't have pity on anyone who was weak. And the other girls would only make fun of her.

Nancy placed the head of her sleeping bag as

far away from the trees as possible and then carefully unzipped it, checking every inch for a hidden insect. When she was satisfied that it was clean, she slipped her body inside and zipped up the bag all the way, even though the night was hot and sticky. She lay there, staring up at the moon, thinking about all the insects that might be crawling across the ground toward her. In her mind, they became like an army — spiders with long spindly legs, ants with bulging eyes, beetles with hard bodies, millipedes with thousands of creepy legs. After what seemed like hours of this waking nightmare, Nancy finally fell asleep.

Her own scream woke her up. At first she thought she was screaming in a nightmare — the worst nightmare she'd ever had. She was dreaming that a huge insect was covering her face and biting her. But then she realized that the scream was real and some horrible thing *was* on her face, biting her. In a panic, she twisted out of her sleeping bag and frantically brushed off her face.

It was early dawn, and her scream had woken up the other girls. They were staring at her with sleepy, scared eyes. Nancy saw that all their eyes were fixed on her right cheek. It was stinging. She quickly raised her hand to the spot and felt a large bump that itched and was hot. It was a bite. An insect bite.

Nancy screamed again and started to brush off

all over her body. She was terrified that the insect was still on her. The other girls started to laugh at her and point at the red spot on her face. Finally, the counselor forced her to calm down and to stop trying to brush away the insect that was no longer there. But, all the rest of the day, Nancy's hand kept creeping back up to her face to feel the horrible, stinging spot.

That night, all the campers went back to the cabin to sleep. But Nancy didn't sleep — not for a long time. She had looked at the bite in the mirror in the camp washroom. It was big and swollen and red. All she could think about was the insect that had bitten her. In her mind it grew bigger and bigger and more frightful-looking. All night long, she kept brushing that insect off her face until just before dawn when she fell asleep.

The next day she went to see the camp nurse about the bite. The nurse examined it carefully and said it wasn't a tick bite. That's all she seemed to care about. She told Nancy to leave the bite alone and it would go away.

But the bite didn't go away. Every day it got redder and redder and bigger and bigger. Everyone at camp stared at it and laughed. And every time they stared, Nancy felt that insect crawling across her face and biting her.

Finally, one evening, Nancy went to the washroom and stood in front of the mirror, staring at the horrible red spot on her face. It was swollen bigger than ever and hurt her cheek. She reached down to the sink and splashed hot water on the spot. Then, all of a sudden, it burst open.

And, while she stared at herself in the mirror, Nancy saw ten little black spiders crawl out of their eggs and scurry across her face.

The Red Bandanna

It was quiet hour. I lay on my bottom bunk thinking about the seven other girls I would be sharing this cabin with for the next two weeks. This morning we had been strangers. But, already, we knew a lot about each other. We knew who was the greediest for food in the dining hall. We knew who was afraid of spiders. And we all knew who would be the outsider in the cabin — Charlotte, the girl in the top bunk above me. Charlotte, with her red bandanna around her neck.

I could hear Charlotte's breathing right now. She must be asleep, I thought, because her breath was coming in long, raspy sounds. I started to grit my teeth together as I listened to that sound, over and over again. I couldn't believe that I had to sleep in the bunk under Charlotte for two whole weeks. It was enough to make me want to go home.

Just then, I heard Liz clear her throat across the cabin from me. I glanced over and caught her eye. She pointed up to Charlotte and then made a choking motion with her hands. We both started to giggle until Laura, our counselor, jumped out of her bunk and came over to give us a mean stare. I went back to reading my book of ghost stories and tried to ignore Charlotte's breathing until quiet hour finally ended.

The counselor had to shake Charlotte awake to get ready for our swimming lesson. We all got into our suits, grabbed our towels, and waited impatiently for Charlotte to join us outside the cabin. When she finally came out, we stared at her in disbelief. She had on her swimming suit, but the red bandanna was still around her neck.

"Charlotte," Laura said, "take your bandanna off and leave it in the cabin. Then we can all get going."

"No," Charlotte said with a determined edge to her voice. "I can't."

Liz and I stared at each other and made big eyes. Charlotte was even stranger than we thought.

Laura opened her mouth to start to say something, but she must have decided not to argue with Charlotte in front of the rest of us. We all headed down to the lake, glancing every once in a while at the red bandanna around Charlotte's neck.

The cold water of the lake felt good because it was a hot and sticky day. We all had races swimming back and forth between the dock and a diving platform about fifty yards out into the lake — all of us but Charlotte. She got wet once, but then just sat on the dock shivering and twisting the ends of the red bandanna around her fingers.

When we went back to the cabin to change, Charlotte still kept on the red bandanna, even though it was wet and soppy. We all started to whisper among ourselves about why she kept it on. Did she have some horrible scar underneath it? Was it some kind of weird security blanket? Liz even came right out and asked Charlotte why she didn't take it off. Charlotte just said, "I can't."

Charlotte became the joke of our cabin. What we did to her wasn't nice, but you know how it is at camp. Somebody always gets picked on. We short-sheeted her bunk. We hid a frog in her duffel bag. We made fun of her raspy breathing at night, imitating her and then laughing until even Laura joined in.

But after three nights of listening to that horrible, raspy breathing, I was at the end of my wits. It was our fourth night in the cabin. The temperature had soared into the high nineties during the day, and the night air was still hot and sticky. I hadn't been able to get a decent night's sleep ever since I'd come, and now I was tossing and turning, listening to Charlotte's breathing.

"Maybe it's that bandanna," I whispered to Liz. "Maybe that's why she makes so much noise when she sleeps."

"Why doesn't she just take it off?" Liz said.

"Why don't we?" I said. "Maybe we could get some peace and quiet then."

"Good idea," I heard Kate say from another bunk.

"Let's see what's underneath it," Mary added in the dark.

Liz started to giggle and said, "Let's do it."

We knew Laura had to be awake, but she didn't let on. She probably wanted to stop Charlotte's noisy breathing as much as we did. And I'll bet she was as curious as we were about what was under the red bandanna.

Liz searched around in the dark for her little flashlight and then handed it to me. Everybody sat up in their bunks to watch as Liz climbed up the side of Charlotte's bunk. I got out of mine and held the flashlight for Liz as she reached over Charlotte's head and started to untie the red bandanna.

I could see that her hands were shaking as she struggled to loosen the knot that held the bandanna tight around Charlotte's neck. I thought that Charlotte would wake up for sure. But her heavy, raspy breathing just went on and on.

Liz finally undid the first knot of the bandanna. Charlotte's breathing suddenly became louder and raspier. It sounded scary. I noticed that the light was quivering now because my hands had started to shake.

But Liz kept on working at the last knot of the bandanna. Everyone had gathered close around to watch. Finally, Liz worked the knot loose, and the red bandanna fell away from around Charlotte's neck. There was a sharp, choking sound in Charlotte's throat, and her eyes suddenly flew open.

Then her head slowly began to roll off her neck. And it fell right off the top bunk onto the floor.

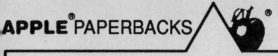